Dry Days, Wet Nights

Maribeth Boelts

Illustrated by

Kathy Parkinson

Albert Whitman & Company, Morton Grove, Illinois

To my family. M.B.
For John, Sarah, and Emily,
with thanks for your cooperation. K.P.

Design by Lucy Smith.

Text copyright © 1994 by Maribeth Boelts.
Illustrations copyright © 1994 by Kathy Parkinson.
Published in 1994 by Albert Whitman & Company,
6340 Oakton Street, Morton Grove, Illinois 60053.
Published simultaneously in Canada by
General Publishing, Limited, Toronto.
Manufactured in Mexico.
10 9 8 7 6 5 4 3 2

Library of Congress Cataloging-in-Publication Data

Boelts, Maribeth, 1964—
    Dry Days, Wet Nights / written by Maribeth Boelts;
illustrated by Kathy Parkinson.
        p.   cm.
Summary: Little Bunny wants to stop wetting his bed at night, and his
parents patiently help him realize that that will happen when the time is right.
        ISBN 0-8075-1723-2 (hardcover)
        ISBN 0-8075-1724-0 (paperback)
        [1. Bedwetting—Fiction. 2. Rabbits—Fiction.] I. Parkinson, Kathy, ill.
II. Title.
PZ7.B635744Dr   1994   93-28674
[E]—dc20   CIP
                                               AC

A Note for Parents

Among preschool-aged children, bed-wetting is very common. Approximately forty percent of three-year-olds, thirty percent of four-year-olds, and fifteen percent of five-year-olds have not achieved nighttime bladder control.

It is important for parents to maintain a low-key, patient attitude toward bed-wetting. Wet bedding and pajamas should be treated casually, as a normal part of the effort toward mastery. Reassure your child that many children wet their beds, and that soon enough he or she will stay dry. When your child does have a dry night, offer praise and maybe a small reward such as a sticker.

There is no single cause for bed-wetting, and medical factors are rarely responsible. After your child reaches school age, if you become concerned about the situation, take your child to a doctor. Once a full evaluation has been completed and medical factors are ruled out, there are several options available for helping the school-aged child.

In *Dry Days, Wet Nights,* Little Bunny's nighttime control develops gradually, just as it does in a great majority of children. You can help your child most during this time by moving on to other things, encouraging and celebrating each step towards maturity.

Little Bunny lined up his four yellow ducks along the edge of the bathtub while Mama laid out his towel and pajamas.

"Mama?" he said. "Can I leave my diaper off tonight? Only babies wear diapers to bed, and I'm not a baby."

"You're certainly not a baby—you stay dry all day," Mama said. "It's the nighttime that is a little hard for you."

"I can try, Mama," LB said.

Mama smiled. "We can see what happens tonight. If your body is ready, then you'll stay dry."

LB worked on the buttons of his flannel pajamas.

"Do you need some help with that top button?" Papa asked.

"I can do it," LB said. "My chin just keeps getting in the way."

LB tilted his chin a bit and pushed the button through the buttonhole in the blue flannel. After he finished dressing, LB brushed his teeth, went to the potty, and hopped into bed.

It was in the black of the night, long
after Mama and Papa's goodnight kisses,
that LB dreamt he was sailing in a hot air
balloon high above his house. It was a grand
dream at first, as LB waved to his friends down below.
But then the balloon kept sailing higher, above the clouds,
and higher, above the planets, and even higher, above all the
stars. Finally, the balloon stopped sailing, and it was just
LB and the balloon and a dark, lonely sky all around.

It was then that LB woke up, cold, wet, and confused.

"Mama?" LB called. "Papa?"

"What is it, Little Bunny?" Mama answered from their
bedroom down the hall.

"Mama, hurry!" answered LB. "My bed is all sweaty, and my pajamas are, too."

Mama's slippers flip-flopped down the hall and into LB's room. She clicked on LB's lettuce lamp. "Oh, it's okay," she said. "You just wet the bed while you were sleeping."

"But I didn't even know I had to go potty," LB said.

"That's because you were sleeping so deeply," Mama said. She helped LB step one leg, then two into soft cotton pajamas.

After Mama changed the sheets, LB climbed back into bed.

"Goodnight, Mama," LB said tiredly.

"Goodnight again, Little Bunny," said Mama.

The next night, LB dreamt that he was standing in the front row at the circus.

He was tossing peanuts to the
elephants when something woke
him up, just a bit—something
that told him he needed to go
to the bathroom.

He opened his eyes a little, and the
circus and the elephants disappeared.
He was standing next to his bed . . . in wet
pajamas. "Mama?" he called.

Mama didn't answer, so LB followed
the glow of the nightlight down the hall
and into Mama and Papa's room. He
whispered in Papa's ear. "I'm wet, Papa."

Papa helped LB into a pair of clean pajamas and wiped up the wet spot next to LB's bed.

"You tried, didn't you?" Papa said, kissing him on the end of his nose.

LB nodded and yawned. "I was dreaming about the circus. I was feeding peanuts to a great big elephant with a long... a long... trunk."

"We went to the circus for your birthday last year, didn't we?" Papa said as he clicked off the lettuce lamp.

"Um-hmm," LB answered, pulling his blanket up to his chin. "I think I'll go back to that dream."

On the third night, LB waited until he was sure that Mama and Papa were sleeping. Then he crept down the long hallway to the bathroom and sat on the shaggy blue rug.

"I'm just going to stay here and wait until I have to go potty," he said quietly. So he waited, and he waited, for what seemed to be a very long time. Soon the shaggy blue rug looked like a comfortable place for a bunny to rest. And before long, LB was curled up sleeping.

The next morning, when LB woke up in his own bed, he knew what must have happened. "I had my clown pajamas on last night, not my cowboys," he said.

For many nights, LB went to bed in one pair of pajamas and woke up in another.

"I'm a baby," LB said one morning at breakfast, poking at his oatmeal with the tip of his spoon.

"No, LB, you're *not* a baby," Mama said. "You're just a young bunny whose body isn't quite ready to stay dry through the night."

LB felt two hot tears slide down his nose.

Papa wiped his face. "LB?" he said.

"Yes, Papa?"

"Did you know that there are lots and lots of other young bunnies who wet the bed, even bunnies who are older than you?" said Papa.

"There are?" LB said.

"Yes. In fact, when I was about your age, I used to wet the bed," Papa said.

"You did?" LB said. "Did you feel like a baby, too?"

"Sometimes I did," Papa answered. "But your grandma and grandpa told me that my body would keep growing and changing, and soon it would be ready to stay dry through the night. And that's just what happened."

Mama spooned some clover honey onto LB's oatmeal.

LB scooped up a bite and asked, "Do you think I should start wearing my diaper again, till I'm ready to stay dry?"

"I don't think so, LB," Mama said. "We don't mind washing your sheets in the morning if you don't mind changing your pajamas in the middle of the night."

"No, I don't mind, I guess," said LB.

Summer came, and Mama, Papa, and LB found lots of other things to do and talk about. There was a bike with training wheels to learn to ride, swimming lessons to take,

and bubbles to blow out on the green grass. LB outgrew two pairs of sneakers, and Mama had to let out the straps on his overalls.

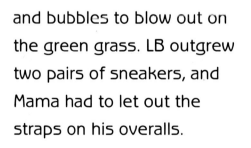

One hot August day, Mama, Papa, and LB went to the county fair. They ate hot dogs and drank blueberry ices and rode the Ferris wheel three times. LB was exhausted when Papa tucked him in that night.

The next morning, LB woke up to the sounds of the neighborhood bunnies already playing at the park across the street.

He stretched and breathed in deeply. Something was different. He felt his sheets, as he always did. They were dry. He looked at his pajamas. They were the same dinosaur ones he had worn to bed the night before. And they were dry, too!

LB ran to the bathroom and went potty. As soon as he had flushed the toilet, he skipped down the stairs to tell Mama and Papa the news.

"Mama!" he shouted. "Papa! Guess what?!"

"What?" they both said.

"I STAYED DRY!" LB said, hugging Papa first and then Mama with the biggest hug he could give.

"You did?" Papa said, laughing. "How wonderful!"

"I'm never going to wet the bed again!" said LB.

"Let's take one day at a time, Little Bunny," Mama said. "And on this day, I think we should celebrate."

And when LB's bed was made, and his dinosaur
pajamas were hung on the hook by his toybox, that's
exactly what they did.